MOVES....

Evincepub Publishing
Nehru Nagar, Bilaspur, Chhattisgarh 495001
First Published by Evincepub Publishing 2020

ISBN: 978-93-90362-54-7
Price: Rs.170/-

MOVES.....

An unbeatable romantic love story...

By

Malavika Reddy

About The Book

'Moves' is an interesting book that holds the hidden things of men, women and their drive and what drives them through sensitive things like love, trust, romance, thoughts, need etc. 'Moves' shows the Understanding of men and women towards their walk of life. 'Moves' includes the diversity of pages, the love of science that hold the sociality of life.

Unbeatable love stories and 'Moves' is a subject of love, friendship, intimacy, sex and much more which speaks about feelings and emotions that people are tied up with. Everyone doesn't just read the lines of this book but understand the moves of life and moreover we should respect it.

Is it a triangular love story? Rather to say triangular, I would say its love and moves of life that make you understand and feel what exactly is love, intimacy, sex or friendship is? When your fingers move on to the pages, you will feel the love of life, and I'm sure you are going to relate to your lives and start loving your lives that's the speciality of moves.

'Moves' is a concept of unbeatable love and immersed love that shows the depth and sensuality of understanding. Catch the moves to know the everlasting essence of sensual things. Open-minded nature, sociality, hidden values form the era of understanding deeper values of men and women... Please go ahead and read this love story that drives your life with passion and love.

It shows the making of bold moves and the commitment of lives. So then why waiting, hold a book in your hand and let me know what you felt after reading it. Heartful thanks everyone for your wishes, blessings, and support. Its an added love always...

About The Author

Malavika Reddy is an inspiring, loving and good-hearted girl. She always makes people understand about the depth of relationships, feelings, love and emotions.

She is a passionate writer and works has a software engineer. She always tells people how to catch the beauty of life through love. And yes, simple and down to earth girl who always says humanity and love come first.

WHAT IS MOVES?

"Moves" is an interesting book that holds the hidden things of men, women, and their drive and what drives them through sensitive things like love, trust, romance, thoughts, needs, etc. "Moves" shows the understanding of men and women towards their walk of life. "Moves" includes the diversity of pages, the love of science that holds the sociality of life.

An unbeatable love story and "Moves" is a subject of love, friendship, intimacy, sex, and much more, which speaks about feelings and emotions that people are tied up with. Everyone doesn't just read the lines of this book but they also understand the moves of life and, we should respect it.

Is it a triangular love story? Rather say triangular? I would say it's love and moves of life that make you understand and feel what exactly is love, intimacy, sex or friendship is? When your fingers move on to the pages, you will feel the love of life and I'm sure you are going to relate your lives to it and start loving your lives too. That's the specialty of "Moves".

"Moves" is a concept of unbeatable love and immersed love that shows the depth and sensuality of understanding. Catch the moves to know the everlasting essence of sensual things. Open-minded nature, sociality, and hidden values form the era of understanding deeper values of men and women...

Please go ahead and read this love story that drives your life with passion and love.

It shows the making of bold moves and the commitment of lives. So then why waiting, hold a book in your hand and let me know what you felt after reading it. A heartfelt thanks to you all for your wishes, blessings, and support. It's an added love always...

To start about the unbelievable love stories. No love story is less or more.

If we can never see the difference in love, every love is the same.

Many characters, many dreams, many views, many thoughts that constitute love. And yes, that's life. Every move forms life.

"Moves" is a subject of love, intimacy, sex, and much more which speaks about feelings and emotions.

What actually is love? Easy word but very tough to explain and yes, one who can experience it only can feel that.

Love is life and yes we need to be happy always. That is what makes life beautiful. Who likes to experience pain always? Pain in love is too, beautiful but not always good.

When we see the confidence and love in someone's eyes, I say go ahead and yes to choose the life you want. It is always the best thing that can happen in life.

Here I introduce Aish i.e. Aishwariya, her beauty holds her name. And yes very ambitious, independent girl, full of love, beauty, well behaved and brainy too.

Loyal to her love and life.

She was pursuing her higher studies and unfortunately, lost her mother at a very young age and what happened next was not that okay .i.e. with her stepmom. Her stepmom was also beautiful but not that loving, rather she was always calculative.

Her dad was her strength and everything for her. Aish was tall and her features were like no less than a model. She was also very good-hearted and yes, a very bold and beautiful girl. She was outspoken and the special thing about her was that her eyes were full of love.

Aish had to go to college. Aish baby was running to catch the bus. Sometimes she liked to travel by bus though she knew driving. But sometimes, she had to catch the bus to reach college.

She had tied high pony with little sweat slowly touching her eyes. She wiped it and breathed a little deep and caught the bus finally. She had completed her graduation in B.Com and currently, was pursuing her M.Com. She was studying in Delhi but her native place was Bombay.

Bombay, the most commercial place where life starts in Bombay after midnight.

It was a place for lots of business and the temperature was hot always. We can see the mix of poor and most rich people who have settled there.

She always loved to stay in Bombay because most of her studies started there. She had returned to Delhi for her holidays.

Though her choice was to have the mouth-watering pizza and burger but to have street-side food was her favorite.

She was a very modern girl with modern thoughts. Her dressing sense was too good with a t-shirt and jeans sometimes. Most of the time, she wore knee-length skirts and sleeveless frocks.

Aish always wanted her nails to be clean and trimmed and she never liked applying nail polish to her nails.

She always wanted to have a natural look without lipstick. She insisted that girls should be natural, neat than applying makeup.

She had met her friend, Mottu who was a little fat and one of her best friends who accompanied her to have chats and ice-cream together, to talk and share all the things that were hidden and yes, chit-chatting with a friend after a long time makes a girl's face blush with happiness and yes, they shared a good friendship.

Friends are the ones who understand more than loved ones and it's true in any love story. They support anyone's love with a dedication which is the true meaning of friendship.

Aish had very less friends and she was very peculiar in choosing people.

So her circle was less with minimal friends. She had a boyfriend who was smart and his name was Akash. He was a good guy and life was going smooth.

Suraj and Aish had a common friend, Rupa. Rupa and Aish had planned to go to Singapore on a trip with four for their friends including Akash. That was a nice and memorable trip with a photo session. Akash and Aish were standing beside the statue while Rupa and Suraj were standing next to them.

Rupa was a good and average looking girl. Suraj was outspoken and yet a kind of shy person.

Suraj's dream was to have a loving life and he carried his love where ever he went.

Suraj was a romantic person who always dreamt of love. Love was everything to him in life.

Suraj had lost his mother at a very young age and his father was doing business.

He had a sister and his stepmom always loved the daughter more than her son.

She was pampered and was good at her studies and her name was Prerana.

Prerana was a shy, very authentic, pampered daughter with a lot of love. She was worried about being beautiful sometimes. A Little fat with specs, she was a very mature girl with her thoughts who always corrected Suraj whenever he was wrong.

Suraj never liked someone feeling inferior about themselves and always supported his sister.

But somewhere he was thinking what if he had been gifted with the same love as his sister and the way she was pampered. Suraj was doing his higher studies abroad and was a damn romantic guy.

Suraj's mother was always concerned about Suraj settling down with a nice job but he always wanted to be a great businessman and was striving very hard for that.

He was playing cricket well and had won the many cups in cricket. He was a nice batsman and an all-rounder.

He was a good dancer and "live your life as you wish" was his saying about life.

And he used to spend time with dear ones as they always wanted him beside them.

He was very, very charming, and would catch everyone's attention with his smile, love, and talk. Somewhere he was lacking in mother's love. With his stepmom, he did feel support and love yet he felt that insecurity many times.

His stepmom was talkative, bold, and strict

with her words and actions.

She supported him whenever he was wrong and allowed him to have more fun and that was when Suraj would enjoy his life to the ultimate.

Meeting new friends, partying, and enjoying in pubs was common for him.

Every weekend he was catching friends, discussing life, career, etc.

And yes, when guys talk they always have fun.

He was addicted to playing rummy, cards with friends. Sometimes betting was common in his friends' circle including him.

God was also jealous of his enjoyment, such was his rocking life.

Midnight parties and boozing was quite common for him. But everything was in limits. He never took too many drinks apart from one or two pegs.

Suraj was a nice listener of his friends' stories which they use to share while boozing. The terrible love stories, career success, and failure stories and their effects.

One thing was common in their friend circle that if anyone was in depression or failure in love then they will arrange a party immediately, booze enough, console them, and fill them with confidence. And Suraj was nice at it.

He was a travel freak and was used to travel a lot, photography was his hobby and interest.

His sense of taking pictures was so outstanding. His taste was too good and it was like he had wheels in his legs since traveling was his passion.

Understanding the world through travel

was his mindset. He had got many scolding for that from his parents and Aish always.

Everyone, I will tell you to know how Suraj fell in love with Aish and how much he tried to make Aish love him.

The memorable trip made him feel like Aish was the only girl that he needed in his life and her taste, love, thoughts were deeply rooted in Suraj's heart.

Though Aish already had a boyfriend, Suraj tried his best in gaining her attention and making her love him.

On that trip, he was watching Aish every minute and his eyes were so strong that he wanted to catch her and keep her close to his eyes.

What else can I say, whether it was the poor guy Akash who let his girl go without any option or it was Suraj who was very strong in making Aish feel his love with that made her fall for him without thinking twice.

Aish was a very, very intelligent girl with beauty and brain. She had published many papers on her subjects.

Suraj was like a quiet, normal guy and charming too but after he met her, his attitude, dressing, and choices became very specific.

He made himself look so handsome that every girl would dream of him and his talk would leave every girl will dreaming of having such a person in life.

Aish had joined a wonderful university to pursue her higher CA studies and Suraj had joined her in completing his MS.

He finally made Aish love him and was very possessive about her.

They started loving each other, shared their past, and started speaking about their families. One thing was common in both of them of having a stepmom. They shared their feelings about it always.

They were missing mom's love from the core of their heart.

But this situation made them love each other deeply. So much that they were not able to even think of leaving each other.

She made him give his best in everything and her smile was his charm. She used to love every photo-shoot he did.

Since she was a very ambitious girl, she made him come out of his fear and shy nature. His food habits, eating habits got completely changed.

The way he talked, ate, everything was seen in his behavior. "Nothing in this world is bad and we should experience everything", was his life saying.

Aish had bought that kind of a change and he was giving his best in everything as a result of which, she started loving him so heartfully.

Suraj was a very helpful guy and helped his friends always with money and other kinds of support. He gave moral support to his friends always.

Suraj worked in some stores to clear his loan and for his survival on a part-time basis.

Aish was a “no compromise” attitude girl in everything. Everything should be like how she wishes and Suraj was okay with everything for his baby. He saved her name as “baby” in his phone.

They used to meet each other often with friends and staying in friends’ homes,

arranging drinks and playing cards, playing truth or dare was common.

His friends knew that they were in love

and always heard comments "made for each other" from their friends. Late-night staying was common.

That was a fantastic cricket match in college and Suraj started batting. It was a wide, again it was wide and the third time he hit four.

Suraj hit six continuously one after another four times on spin balls.

Aish was so happy and finally, he won the match.

With Cup in his hand, he was very happy and it showed on Aish's face

Aish always wanted Suraj to win everything and her support was enormous in making him learn many things.

Aish always had an intelligent talk with Suraj and he always loved it. Every call of hers was a memory to cherish when recalling many things.

Suraj used to say that there is no friend without selfish nature. There will be one or the other thing or help or need in their mind and that's what is true he felt.

Suraj always used to help Aish and supported her so much whenever she needed it.

Suraj used to go to the gym every day. His everyday workouts were good and he maintained it well.

Aish had perfect beauty, brain, and manners. She carried herself well.

Sometimes her dressing sense made Suraj insecure and he was very protective and possessive about her. She always wore beautiful skirts and frocks.

She was a very punctual girl and she maintained her nice timing. Perfection was her style.

They had many pizzas and burgers together that made their love.

It didn't take that much time for them to fall in love and that was a beautiful evening. They had gone on a cruise and the ocean looked amazing, full of blue color and they were holding hands and looking at the island where they were completely making love and that was the place of their first kiss ever. They cherished their love always with that memory of making it again and again.

After a few days, they met at home. When you are in love everything seems perfect and right. He was a hot guy and he held her tight in his arms covering her waist. Her chest got pressed to his body. They started breathing high and continued kissing each other deeply. Their love synced as her lips started shying away a little.

He pulled her so tight that she hugged him and he slowly carried her and took her to bed. With his hands on her waist kissing her navel, he slowly started kissing her fingers and started licking it and removed her top. He held her head tight and smooched her more strongly. They started undressing each other slowly, and completely. With one hand, he removed her brazier and kept it aside and touched her boobs, kissed her tits, and kissed her whole body. Finally, he pulled her legs apart and they made for each other. They had very sensual intercourse.

Suraj was a very hot guy and both felt sex as a part of love. They made love many times whenever they stayed together.

Though she was insecure about the future, she was more worried about Suraj's future and financial stand up for him which was very necessary since they were studying still.

Once Aish had fled down to Bangalore and had visited Suraj's home.

She got ready and they went to Nandi hills for a photo session.

The weather was awesome and Aish was dressed in a long red gown with a Printed blouse and Suraj captured wonderful images of her. Then they gave the camera to someone asking to take their pictures together.

Suraj had many folders of only Aish's pictures on his cell phone. He saved it in a hard drive.

Prerana and her mom knew about Suraj's love. Prerana always supported him. But Aish was two years elder than him and that made her always think about their marriage and their settling down.

Years flew and Suraj completed his studies

and started searching for a job. Aish was still pursuing her CA studies. They loved each other very deeply and couldn't stay without each other. They were true partners and shared everything.

Many times Aish fought with him for partying hard and traveling more. She was feeling very lonely without him.

Her only concern was marriage and she was waiting for that big day.

Somehow he managed to be with her for two years and finally, Suraj's father was after him and warned him that if he didn't come back he would come there himself.

Without option and with a heavy heart, he had to leave Singapore and come to INDIA. They fought for love and Suraj promised Aish that he will return after two years and will marry her.

After he came back to India, Aish had skipped her periods and after 2 months Aish conceived, it was positive.

She repeatedly called him and asked him to get married soon since she was pregnant. Since he was young and had not settled down he messaged her to abort.

Aish lost complete trust in life. She felt cheated and made herself understand that her belief on him led her to that stage.

Suraj was not able to accept the fact nor leave her alone in that condition nor could he tell his parents about it.

Suraj's parents were waiting for him to come back to INDIA and settle down. But Suraj was not able to give up love like that nor leave Aish.

He stopped picking her calls and avoided her and tried to concentrate on different things like cricket and more on business. But there was hardly a second that he could forgive himself nor forget her. He repented for what he did but was helpless.

It was a rainy day and he was thinking about Aish and missing her a lot.

After looking at the message, she completely lost trust in life itself and she went to McDonald's, sat there cried a lot. The boy working there offered her a burger and asked to console herself and said that life won't be the same and she will have better days ahead.

With a lot of uncertainty, the relationship was little sinking and floating with a lot of love.

He avoided her for a few months that lead to a year or so. Later again they started messaging and he was taking care of her.

They spoke in early mornings and every morning he was very particular about picking her call. He made time for her calls and with the uncertainty of life, love was shrinking and he had lost the confidence of getting married to her.

Sometimes he was thinking that maybe with time everything will be consoled as time is the ultimate thing that gets happiness and everything.

Since Suraj was just 25, he desperately wanted to be a businessman and improve his career but his parents wanted him to settle down with some decent job.

Suraj was like a professional, he had to settle down first and then comes the marriage thought.

Aish was a few times comparing her life with her friends' life and was fighting with Suraj. She always had the upper hand and in every fight, Suraj used to fall to her knees and apologized to convince her.

It was very hard for both of them to leave each other after staying together for a long time.

And yes, distance played a major role in their love. He was back in Bangalore and he was missing Aish so much, he suffered a lot.

He faced many health problems and Aish was also very emotional and missed him a lot. Nothing was going in sync.

Suraj got a decent job though not a very good one. Aish used to call him early morning and they used to talk with each other.

Long-distance relationships are so beautiful that you get to know how much you will be dependent on each other and how difficult it is to stay without each other but for Suraj, life was getting complicated day by day staying without her.

Her absence killed him mentally and made him weak though he was trying to come out of it. He concentrated more on cricket so that at least little time will pass without thinking of her but there was no escape and it made him feel low many times.

A professional settle up was a big headache for him as his parents were stressing him a lot since he had graduated 2 years back. Somehow he was managing everything.

As days passed, taking care of Aish turned out to be a still bigger headache. Aish was worried about marriage and she was fighting for it. Aish stopped picking Suraj's calls sometimes to make him understand about marriage and commitment.

And Aniruddh was Suraj close friend and accompanied him in all trips and shared everything with him. They were business partners as well.

Suraj's parents were not at all ready for inter caste marriage. Their castes were different, the tradition was different, customs were different, and the language was different.

And another reason was she was two years elder than him which was a major concern for their parents. She was very modern and all these things made him feel low sometimes.

Once while playing cricket he had a muscle cache and he couldn't play as well due to that.

And he also had a spinal problem which led to terrible back pain. He went to a doctor and took the treatment.

Love has the strength to do anything and everything and I do always stress to be careful and lucky enough to have a loved one who might be a soul mate, friend, parents, sister, or brother or well-wisher. Do love guys and see how beautiful life will be?

Life is beautiful guys and girls it's all about time. Everyone will get good times and worst times as well, but we need to balance it with maturity. That's very important.

Some love stories lose their balance in the maturity of handling things. So I always say do love but be responsible and mature enough.

Aish was a very jealous girl. She couldn't take any girls' comments, likes on Suraj's pictures. She was very possessive.

Two years passed and it was the New Year and Suraj was celebrating his new year with one of his friends.

Aish was missing everything. Suraj lost

control of losing her so much and was very emotional. He couldn't bear the pain and was not able to share it with anyone.

He took green tea to relax and he was dipping the sachet three-four times and threw it without having it. Perhaps that's how love hurts and it's more painful.

She had called him and they spoke for more than an hour on Skype and he was ok i.e. She was a salsa dancer and her passion was dance. They danced well together. Her moves were his love and her love was his stand.

Love is unbeatable and yes we need to face many things and problems when in love.

Once for holidays, she had come down to Delhi. Suraj met her and they both hugged so tight that Suraj started kissing her forehead.

Tears flew from her eyes and she was very

emotional.

They sat down spoke for some one hour and had food together. She had asked the cook to prepare special dishes for Suraj and she starting serving.

He rested for some time and in the evening, he took her to have some chats.

They walked holding hands with her head resting on his shoulder with all fingers interlocked. They met Mottu and had chats with her.

They were laughing for some time looking into the Mottu jokes alias Joshna.

Suraj and Aish returned home. She opened the door and gave the keys to him.

She was preparing tea and he slowly held her and hugged her with resting her legs on his legs they kissed each other deeply. They made love and poured the tea into a single cup and both of them had it.

Aish took a shower and her perfume spread the aroma in the entire room that drew his attention.

There was a lot of foreplay and then what else, he tightly held her, pushed her to the bed kissed her strongly, turned her and moved her hair sideways, and kissed her back. Turned her again kissed her ears and then her neck. She was completely in love and closed her eyes.

They undressed each other went naked and he put his hand on her chest slowly and kissed her whole body, held her legs, and sucked her fingers. She slowly started

spreading her legs. It got erected for him and he lifted her legs, kept on his shoulder and touched her vagina with his fingers, and put his finger inside it. She got aroused and he inserted his penis into her vagina. It was an unbeatable experience of love...

He was upon her body and fucked her continuously for more than fifteen minutes and after some time it was an intense love breathing high that they smooched each other deeply with her lips completely sinking into his lips for ten minutes and that was a greater smooch ever.

They got tired and looked upon the roof and experienced a satisfying love and more important is that love with sex is fine but not sex or only intercourse for pleasure. Here it was love going intimate and physical with a commitment of marriage.

They made such a memorable love and

covered themselves with a blanket slowly and fell asleep hugging each other.

It was early morning and he kissed her forehead and bought her a cup of tea. They shared it and he was damn romantic as always.

They took a shower together and had lunch outside. He spoke to Aish dad and convinced him that he will get engaged soon. Since he spent three days with her he had to return back to his home.

He was relaxed much more than at any time. He was happy like he somehow convinced his father and postponed the marriage for next year after the engagement.

To get the best things in the world you need to experience the worst things and yes they had suffered a lot while staying apart for

3 years.

They always had an idea of settling abroad after marriage. Aish was very particular about it but Suraj was not so sure since he had to convince his parents for the marriage.

Suraj's job wasn't that good he was striving hard to settle down. He joined the night shift in a software company that was disliked by his parents.

Aish had returned to Singapore for her CA. Months flew and Suraj started missing her and his parents were forcing him to get married.

He had joined a new company and it was in night shifts. He became friends with his colleagues Sinchana, Prathibha, and Ramesh.

He got a call from his mom and she started shouting at him stating that it was Thursday that day and told him not to have non-veg. He agreed for that and stopped himself from having to listen to his heart.

Again he got a call, "What mom?" he replied rudely as he was not in a mood to answer her call or listen to her.

Had ordered food in a hotel and was waiting for it to get served. He showed a girl's photo to Sinchana and told that she is working in the same company in a different branch "Do you know her?" he asked She said no...

His mom asked him by the way who he was talking to and asked him if he checked the girl's photos and he said, "I'm checking will get back to you later."

Later he called his mom and said that he has seen the photo but showed his dislike of marrying her.

One day Aish had called and she was pissed by this commitment and started shouting at him badly with high tone and her tears flew unstoppably.

He consoled her and wished on her birthday and he missed calling her and it was she who had called him and started talking.

He was very careful about the emotions they had and spoke for about three to four hours.

He left his work and went to the washroom and spoke to her for a long time. While he returned, he could see his eyes full of tears.

Love is not just an infatuation, sexual pleasure, or only a responsibility. It's a commitment and we need to manage it with enough maturity and hold a relationship with all love and that's how it should be...

Months passed and he became close to his office colleagues. Outings were common and it was a great relaxation for him to spend with them. They became great friends.

He always loved Sinchana more than anything for her love.

She was silent and such a beautiful girl that he always loved her more. Slowly he felt a girl should have those qualities that make life beautiful and not just being beautiful and it's not only the external beauty that matters.

But the internal good wishes, prayers, and clean hearted love are all that people should hold on to.

She was such a mesmerizing beauty with deep clear eyes. Her dressing sense was amazing. Sometimes being simple and sometimes with bright colors and whenever she left her hair, she was looked like a goddess on earth who came to show how beautiful life is...

Suraj always thought there was no other girl beautiful than Aish.

But once he met Sinchana he was clean bold for her warm love and when he looked into her eyes every time, he lost himself and was dreaming about what a soulful beauty she is ?

Sometimes Suraj used to tease her with songs and was waiting to see her daily since she was such a charm of erasing all pain and filling life with colors.

Prathibha was on leave the next day. Every day they had tea, coffee once they entered office.

Ramesh, Sinchana, and Suraj went to have coffee and tea. Sinchana and Suraj walked together always and sometimes Sinchana first and then Suraj.

They shared a very good relationship. Staircase walking was their favorite.

Before Suraj could tell anything about his life to Sinchana. She had guessed it by observing his behavior because she had seen his smile, tears, and understood his heart. No other girl in her place could have guessed so well.

Sinchana got a call and was shocked and said "What?"

It was Prathibha with full of low voice and tears. Days back they had attended her wedding.

They couldn't forget the way she was looking so bright and full of smiles. She was shocked to listen to her saying that she would not come to the office and perhaps she would resign and ended the call.

Sinchana tried calling many times in ten minutes and Prathibha didn't pick up the call.

By then, Suraj and Ramesh had finished their coffee.

Suraj started having coffee a few times apart from having green tea always. It was Aish who always insisted to have green tea and told him to have capsicum slices which were good for muscles.

And she had a habit of reading things and to know recent news and made Suraj also do the same.

He always obeyed her words and followed them. In one way he was missing her, on the other way, life was very good with his friends. Never give up for love was his mindset and was okay if Aish has a better future than him.

As friends, they enjoyed a lot and they were few guys who boozed horribly though Suraj was accompanying them he never took more than a sip.

Oh god, if they hold the glass they never kept it down. Continuously one after the other and Sinchana with others felt that if alcohol was water then these people would have survived by having it leaving food and taking alcohol has food.

They went for many trips with a lot of pictures captured by Suraj and others.

Pictures were too good and they were girls who posed for selfies so much.

And sometimes Suraj loved taking pics with them just to make Aish feel jealous.

Aish was a beauty with brain and never liked it and was always jealous of it.

She was not that interested in social media or posting pictures. She was busy with her exams and many things.

Suraj had told about Aish to his mom and his mom was not that happy because of caste and many things though she liked the girl.

Suraj was upset with his mom's decision and it was sad to see a fun-loving guy being sad sometimes.

To the core, his life was filled with fun, fun, and fun. And dealing with emotions and feelings was like handling tough times.

The next day in the office Sinchana was sad and Suraj took her to have coffee.

His eyes were melting if he could see Sinchana dull and that was love stored for her.

Her place in his heart was to that height. He never thought some girl could take such a goddess-like place in his heart.

"Oh, the soulful beauty why didn't I meet you earlier?" was his question to fate many times.

He asked Sinchana why she was so dull and Sinchana's eyes were filled with tears. She told that Prathibha was not picking the call and she was going to leave the job.

He said, "We will meet her directly by going to her house and we will talk because I think something is serious."

They logged out and Suraj said we will go in a car to Prathibha's place and ask her what happened? Sinchana said, "What about Ramesh?" Suraj looked into her eyes and she got to know he was accompanying for breaks but not so close so not required.

They reached Prathibha's place and her mom welcomed them saying namaskara which means hi and called Prathibha loudly.

She came down. Though she was dull, she smiled and bought them coffee. Sinchana and Suraj were happy for her and thought that everything was cool.

They went to the balcony and slowly to her room. Sinchana entered and Prathibha came after her. As soon as she closed her door, she hugged her and started crying loudly.

Suraj was beside and said to relax and asked Sinchana to get some water.

She ran down and asked auntie for water and she gave a bottle out of the fridge and Sinchana made her drink some water and tapped her head slowly and hugged her for some time.

It was a silence of fifteen minutes that made them think 1000 things and finally, Prathibha said everything is over and Sinchana replied, "What? What is over? You are newly married and you should be happy. So smile, please.

Every problem has a solution and you need not cry like this baby."

"Relax baby and let us know what happened." She started telling her story and Sinchana sat on her bed with wood support at the back making her lying down on lap and pampering her with love...

Bhargav is giving divorce to me Sinchana. He was my seven years of love.

Sinchana asked why?

Prathibha told them that he didn't like her.

Sinchana said, "What happened, he was good at marriage?"

Suraj asked "Fucker, why not? He was happy on the marriage day and said that's why Sinchana I don't believe in marriages. There is no commitment."

Sinchana told Suraj to relax let Prathibha tell.

Sinchana told Prathibha, "Relax, now you don't think about anything and take rest for some fifteen days."

Prathibha asked, "How shall I tell my parents about this truth and it's a love marriage. I was completely responsible for this. They will be hurt a lot."

Sinchu told Prathibha, "We will go for a trip

and we will talk there and find a solution?"

Outings always make us relaxed and we can think better.

Suraj gave a hi-fi to Sinchana for her graceful solution and Sinchu wiped Prathibha tears. She made her have breakfast and stayed there for 2 hours and was about to leave.

Prathibha asked, "How is the office?" Sinchu replied, "Haan it's going good but missed you and your g-talks. She smiled..."And Suraj caught her smile and paused like it was his action. Sinchu told, "I'm not going to the office tomorrow since I have some work."

Suraj thought, "Oh no angel, how will I stay without seeing you nor talking to you."

"You don't come with a story or a call," everyone started laughing loudly.

Prathibha fell to the bed and started laughing loudly.

Sinchu was very happy and Suraj told, “Who the fucker he is to take away your Smile. We will see what can be done till then please smile and come on hugg me tight.”

Prathibha lied down on his shoulder for five minutes and Sinchu thought, “Oh god, what a charming person he is... He didn’t get back her smile or make her laugh but it was like he got back her life....”

Sinchu for a minute thought, “What if I get a person like him…” and started dreaming.

Suraj interrupted her thoughts saying, “Hello angel ...hello angel,” and said “what are you dreaming?

“What? You need a person like me?” She said yes in her eyes and he said oh no I’m waiting come we will go...lets love.

Sinchu told enough of flirting...

Suraj asked, “You are calling me a flirt?”

She said, “Enough,” hit his head with love and said “let's leave”

Sinchu said bye to Prathibha and they left.

Suraj said, “What you call Prathibha such a big name always. Let’s us start calling her by nickname...”

“What to keep?” asked Suraj

Sinchu had an idea...

“We will call her baby. What will I do with my baby then...oh no”

They started laughing so much so was their friendship...

Suraj asked her left or right, Sinchu replied

right and she knew what was right though we feel for thousand more than anything...

Suraj dropped her home and he reached his home.

That was a hectic day in the office. "Sinchu, please come" called Maansi. She told, "Yea coming..."

"What?" Sinchu asked and Maansi replied, "I have one request and you are not able to understand."

Maansi got up and Sinchu pulled her chair and sat looking deeply into the request.

"By the way, guys and girls in software have usernames and whoever needs something log request through the tool, and that's called a ticket."

Maansi told, “It’s done, haan you’re good that's why I call always and you give me a solution always.”

After a hectic day, they went for dinner she had planned for dinner.

Sinchu was showing all the beautiful pictures to Prathibha and Suraj got a call

“Hello,” he said, “dinner?” she asked “Baby I had chapathi” he said slowly in a low voice.

If it was her baby and anyone was there his response to her was less and with low tone.

Something struck Suraj. Though he was on call, he was looking into Sinchu eyes.

She smiled and then he disconnected the call.

To say, in any relationship, sometimes insecurities are common. It depends upon the situation but doesn't mean their love is not pure or truthful.

Imbalances are common in love and we need to handle with maturity. And different people see love in a different view and for me, love is all about trust and life.

And for some, love may be just looking at each other. They may not cross limits for no reason and one more thing guys, if they look into the eyes or body it’s the same. By Heart or mentally you get connected it is the same as physically getting connected. No need to have a physical touch always.

For some infatuation will be more and they get confused with love.

And few people get connected mentally, by heart, and physically making for each other and that's the formation of love.

When you are only looking into physical feeling then it's wrong.

In love kiss, intimacy is common. For few, love is being romantic and intimate.

But on the whole, remember one thing, it should be love that leads to life and not just time pass.

Being limitless is love and reaching that is life.

Experience true love and you're lucky if you get married to your love and if not then don't worry something best will fall into your place.

That was a rainy day and Suraj had a kitten at home which his mom had bought.

He was holding that on lap on his bed and was lost in himself completely.

Basically, he was a damn romantic guy and that day he had lost completely and something was running in his heart continuously.

Difficult to judge but he was experiencing a mesmerizing love.

That was full of josh day in office everyone planned to go to Ooty and they booked a TT and they were around eighteen people who joined.

Sinchu was talking to the driver and was paying money. With handbag on one hand and two-way bag on her back, she cleared payment of the driver that was collected from everyone.

Sinchu called Prathibha, Prathibha twice with full of love and she replied "Yes darling, I'm here coming..."With the kitbag in one hand and holding her purse, Prathibha asked Sinchu "what?"

Sinchu asked Prathibha, “Can you give me two thousand I need it for now.” She gave her the money.

Akshay took a catch and that was nice. The ball was so high and that was such a beautiful catch outside the company and Sinchu called Akshay, “Let's go... come”

Everyone chatting on the road started getting in and Sinchu said to the driver that he could start. Before leaving Sinchu “miss you guys ...have fun, we will be coming back in a car.”

“Anything needed, call me and yes open your windows ...bye guys,” she left.

Suraj called, “angel can you come?”

Sinchu smiled and said coming...

Suraj wore a black T-shirt with googles to

his eyes. Was, as usual, looking very handsome no less than a hero.

And Sinchu was like, "kuch bhi naa kaho" song heroine very polite and beauty of glimpse.

Prathibha with jeans was looking stunning.

Suraj said to Prathibha, “That rascal left you, you are still in that turmeric thread. You please throw it I get pissed off looking into it.”

Sinchu said to Suraj, “Will you please stop, Where are we going and for what she said?”

“Please remember we will discuss and sort it out. We should fix a relationship not break it.”

“Suraj said, “It’s a weird kind of request with no heart and you want to work on that request."

A great fucker with biting his lips slowly started murmuring within himself.

Started the car, changed the gear, and Sinchu told Suraj, "We need to buy some snacks stop somewhere..."And guys on the bus stopped to buy drinks. Suraj stopped a car and joined them.

They took some two boxes of liquor drinks and started smoking.

Sinchu was thinking, "How much they will booze now?" and kept her hand on her forehead.

But one thing, how much ever they booze they were not losing their control.

Should appreciate them seriously she thought. Always fit an fine after boozing so much.

Suraj also smoked but was always in limits like one or two and girls were chatting as usual and went to buy snacks.

Sinchu, Prathibha, and Ramesh got into the car. Suraj held one vodka in his hand and from outside the window asked her please have it with full love.

Sinchu smiled and refused to say no in a lower tone. Angel please he asked twice

Sinchu replied no and Suraj was and he was disappointed.

While driving he asked, "Sinchu, will you drive? Shall I teach you?" She said no.

He was again disappointed and then on a highway, they parked the car sideways and stopped the .

Everyone got down to have chai, coffee on the roadside. Wow and that's the beauty of life.

Midnight on the highway to have coffee was like experiencing heaven on earth

Guys talk started and they started laughing loudly and Sinchu asked "what?"

They said no, no you shouldn't listen to it better stay away.

With hands inside her jacket, she moved towards the girls and started talking.

Sinchu went aside and started dreaming and she was a dreamer and a romantic girl. The only thing in life she expected was life was love and that one love.

What is one love guys and girls? I will let you know...

One love, one love, and that was the love

she dreamt about...

One love, what it is? Read the below lines

"Once given is always lost. The truth is that lost one is

The last one to expect......

Once shared is always cared....but the reality is

Relations can't be repaired...

Once broken can be rendered but

A broken heart can never be blundered...

The heart runs faster than the mind

Where we always fall for feelings...

Always giving shows the heights of loveeee

Sometimes it's better to accept than to expect...

Hold life for feelings.............

Hold the hands for the one who leave their footprints behind

Hope that seven steps together

Leads to steps of success in life...........

Never take back the seven steps............

BECAUSE...........

Once the heart is given

It's been owned by someone

Who controls our Heartbeat?"

Aren't those beautiful lines??

And yes, love for her was "One love" that takes seven steps together and ties the knot with lifelong commitment...

One thing every time, What Suraj used to do was, take a photo of Sinchu whenever she is dreaming and save it on his mobile...

He slowly went to her, called her angel, angel. She was in complete imagination of her love and stood silently observing the dawn...

Everyone over there started laughing so much that she started calling her, "Beladinagle baale"

He pulled her hands and she was like “What Suraj?”

Suraj replied amma Devi matha we have to leave and said you come and dream in the car. She smiled and started laughing

She called Prathibha and they held hands together and left the place.

Life moves are always unpredictable that's what we call life and time are great teachers of life...

Everyone reached Ooty and that was fantastic weather making everyone feel heaven on earth.

By the time they reached, it was evening. Everyone took a shower and gathered to have dinner.

Dishes were mouthwatering and everyone was very hungry and had tummy full.

There were varieties of non-vegetarian stuff and less vegetarian food.

Deserts were awesome and everyone had completely.

After some time guys started smoking having drinks.

"Oh!" they shouted Cheers around twelve glasses with a smile around and started enjoying their time by chit chatting

Prathibha silently went on to the peaceful greenery place and started looking at it for some time.

Sinchu went there and hugged her from the back.

They sat on a bench, Suraj went there and held Prathibha's hand and asked what happened?

Prathibha told even she was shocked to heights.

Suraj asked, "But what happened?"

"Did you people fight for any reason?"

"Is he a psychopath or short-tempered guy? Then why the first day got married the second day saying divorce..?"

Sinchu told Suraj to stop it, let her tell...

"Come-on darling, what happened? Tell us

from the start of your marriage."

"As far as we saw he was happy around and had a wide smile for photos and people around..."

Prathibha said, "Trust me guys, even I don't know. After marriage, the first night was arranged at my house. I went inside. He was sitting on the caught and I gave him a glass of milk.

He kept it aside on the table. It made some annoying sounds. I asked is everything fine? He didn't respond and silence went on for about half an hour...

Then he said this doesn't work out. I'm giving you divorce.

I didn't know what to answer.

I thought he was angry for some reason

and maybe in anger, he is saying all this.

He didn't sleep for some 2 hours and again he said I will send you divorce papers sign it.

I asked him again what happened. He replied saying I'm not interested in this relationship."

Suraj said, "Couldn't you slap him left and right? Fucker, why did he get married?"

He could have said that earlier right before marriage.

"Why end a relationship after marriage? What is his problem?"

Sinchu said to Suraj to calm down...

Sinchu asked Prathibha "Did you ask him if the rituals were not performed well or did he have any dissatisfaction in marriage arrangements?"

Prathibha replied, "You all saw the marriage. It was hard-earned money that was spent around seventeen lakhs and in the city, like there it was a very grand marriage that happened."

Suraj intervened, "I don't think that as the reason."

"Some strong reason might be there. Either to say he might have known something about you which is unknown to you or someone who would have told something about you to him or else he might be interested in any other relationship...."

Prathibha wondered, "Something about me. I don't know what? He knows in and out of me and my family. It was not in a short term relationship, it was seven long years of love.

His sister is such a nice friend of mine and

even she shouted at him for his decision and said she is with me."

Suraj got three missed calls, he saw and kept it inside. The fourth time it was ringing.

It was his baby calling and Aish was not disturbing Suraj by calling him repeatedly nor disturbing kind. She had a fixed timing and maintained that.

The fifth time it was ringing and Suraj said 1 second I will call you back and Aish was frustrated already that Suraj was not talking to her properly these days and avoiding her and yes he did so...

Sinchu asked Prathibha, "By the way did you have in dinner?"

Prathibha replied, "I will always have with you people only, oh ya I came searching for you but you weren't there and I thought you were in the bathroom and will join for dinner."

"Later in that tiredness of traveling, I forgot to ask? I came searching for you and you were here..."To make Prathibha smile Suraj said, "Look Prathibha, she so tired. Damn, she drove the car and changed the gear, my god... My angel is tired today..."

Prathibha started laughing and Suraj joined her to look at her...

Sinchu told enough monkey, come we will go... let her first have dinner.

Prathibha finished her food and Sinchu bought dessert to serve Prathibha and

Prathibha was like no... Sinchu please have…

Suraj said, "Look Prathibha she is asking only you, for me?"

"Go monkey you aren't tired right... I will have on behalf of you was her reply..."

Sinchu with her one hand was repeatedly tying her free hair which was falling to her cheeks and touching her lips and Suraj observed it and tied her hair.

She suddenly looked into his eyes and they had eye contact for a minute and thought in mind she is a mesmerizing beauty...

Sinchu had half of the sweet and Suraj had rest of the sweet with the same spoon.

That was the first time they had sweet together and that was the most memorable experience.

Prathibha had her dinner. They sat down in a balcony and starting talking.

Suraj asked in seven years of love had you

noticed any dual minded feelings in him.

"No, Suraj" said Prathibha. "I think so maybe he is interested in another girl...that's my guess ..."

Sinchu asked Prathibha, "Did you guys have lunch and dinner together on the marriage day?"

"Yes" answered Prathibha

"So was he fine on marriage day?"

"Yes"

"What else you spoke on your first night?"

Prathibha told, "Bhargav didn't want to disappoint me by telling earlier looking into the marriage arrangements and waited till first night to convey his decision..."

Sinchu said, "What? Idiot he is..."

Suraj added, "What rubbish? He could you

told you earlier. Isn't it a heartbreak now!!

What kind of rascal he is? Enjoyed the wedding and speaking bullshit about it.

If he had a concern he would have told you earlier and wouldn't have spoiled your life?"

Sinchu agreed, "Yes Suraj, that's right..."

Sinchu told Prathibha, "I don't think he is the right kind of person.

Prathibha you need to be very strong in accepting the facts..."

Prathibha replied Sinchu, "It was a seven-year old relationship. My mind and heart had accepted him as a husband."

"Yes, I agree," Sinchu answered. "But look, seven years doesn't matter if he is breaking a relationship in a single day."

Suraj asked Prathibha, "Are you scared of

anything?"

"What? I didn't get you..."

"I mean about any of your moves with him?"

"It's not about getting scared but how shall I live without him..."

Suraj said to Prathibha "Shall I ask you one question?"

"Yes, of course..."

"How was your relationship with him?"

"It was nice, we were very loving..."

"I mean, how was your intimate relationship? Did you guys have any problem with that? Don't mind, all these matters..."

"We didn't have an intimate relationship..."

"So it was more of emotional bonding..."

Sinchu asked, “Are you sure you didn't cross your limits?”

Prathibha was in silence for two minutes...

“Speak Prathibha...”

Suraj said, “Wait Sinchu... let her take her time.”

Prathibha with closing her hands on her eyes and cried loudly

Suraj told Sinchu to get her some water and told Prathibha to relax.

Sinchu brought a bottle of water and gave it to her.

Sinchu keeping her hands on her waist and looking at Prathibha face and felt very sad...

Suraj said, “Calm down Prathibha, I understand”

Prathibha rested on Suraj’s shoulder

The silence went on for 10 minutes...

Suraj asked "Prathibha, did you have an intimate relationship? That's what is worrying you?"

Prathibha told, "It's not like intimate but, but..."

"What but, but? Come on, tell us."

"We have kissed each other twice."

"Oh god, that is the only concern you have?

"Look Prathibha, having emotional bonding, sharing our feelings, and going intimate is common in love and its life moves and basically it's the moves of love...

Moreover, everything should be a part of love not just infatuation or just pleasure

It happens in any relationship but listen, you should be his love girl...

You should be his girl forever. If that's not the case then no point in thinking..."

"Prathibha, anything apart from that?"

"No nothing ..."

"Don't worry girl, you're very clean like a green do not to think much...

Life is all about accepting the facts, think about your future

Take a bold move. Sign it and throw the divorce papers on to his face...

Start a new life and from this minute you have to forget rather than forgiving him

And have courage and hope..."

Sinchu agreed, "Yes that's right. It should be one love"

Prathibha said, "One more thing"

"Yes please"

"Yes, he likes another girl..."

"Didn't I tell you earlier only? Even if you didn't wish to tell, I could make out.

Perfectly forget what shit happened in your life..."

Sinchu was shocked

"How bold he is to say that after marrying you and having a long term relationship...

When did he tell you that?

After fifteen days of marriage, we had got separated and a day back I had got a call from him and he said that"

"Who is she?"

Prathibha told, "She was his ex-college."

"How does that matter when the

relationship has the test of time...?"

"Forget, forget, forget...and that's all I say"

It was 2 pm, Suraj bought a glass of wine...

And asked Prathibha to have

Sinchu asked, "What Suraj?"

Suraj said, "You girls are like orthodox thinking in everything. Be broadminded girls and most open-minded in your thoughts..."

There is nothing wrong with having a glass of wine.

It makes you relaxed and it's important at this point in time, have it Prathibha...

Prathibha without thinking for a minute had it and held the glass tight

Suraj said "Relax, I understand your emotional bonding with him. Emotionally getting connected takes time to forget..."

And asked, “Shall I offer you one more glass?”

Prathibha answered in affirmative

Suraj cheered her saying, “Cheers girl, stay strong....”

Prathibha smiled, “And yes this smile should make him repent in future that he lost you...”

Sinchu supported, “Yes that's right!”

Suraj phone starting ringing, Sinchu look your baby is calling...

“That’s okay I will talk to her later...”

Suraj, thought, “Baby is in the wrong mood and mad at me.

If I pick the call then again we r going to fight and she will be upset...”

He asked Sinchu, “Can you help me?

“What?”

Pick up the call and say he is not well or he has slept off.

“What?

What if she asks who I am?”

“She knows about you?

I have told her about you many times....”

Sinchu picked the call.

Aish answered, “Hello...”

No response

Aish again said, “Hello”

Sinchu was silent for a second

“Hello”

Sinchu answered, “Hello, sorry baby.”

"What Baby?"

Sinchu said, "Sorry Aish, Suraj is not well. He has slept off."

"His phone is not with him?"

Sinchu said, "Haan"

She closed the cell phone with one hand and said, "Suraj, she is asking why is cell not with him?"

"Tell her that he had put for charge and forgot to take his phone..."

Sinchu told the same

"Ok, ask him to take care.

May I know where you are?"

Sinchu: again closing the phone with her hand and telling Suraj she is asking where you are?

"Tell her in her heart," Sinchu was blank and Suraj looked into Sinchu's eyes

"Tell her, in Ooty"

Sinchu answered as she was told

Aish's anger beeped her in. She disconnected without saying anything.

Aish in her mind talking to herself, "He will be having time to go to Ooty... stupid!

Don't know how is he now? Let that angel only take care. He doesn't get time to talk to me nor be with me?"

Aish didn't call for fifteen days and was in anger and didn't pick up his call nor was online in social networking sites...

She packed her bags and planned to visit Dubai with her friends...

As planned, she went to Dubai with three

of her friends.

Suraj called her again, she didn't pick the call.

It was almost thirty days and whenever they fought Suraj was the first person to go on to his knees and ask sorry...

He was missing her day by day and the relationship was getting complicated.

He texted her, "Baby, I'm sorry..."

One more thing, he was worried always about her clothes, whenever she packed her bags she used to show him her clothes which she was going to wear...

Suraj was possessive about her wearing short clothes in his absence and was insecure but Aish liked modern dressing always...

Suraj was tensed about what Aish was

doing? Where is she?

Then later, in social media one of her friends tagged Aish and she was in Dubai...

Suraj climbing the stairs was upset and the mood was of...

Later somehow it got patched up and they started talking to each other...

On-call Aish said, "Ooty was nice to you... a girl was beside you to take care."

Suraj, got angry and said, "Yes... she is my angel..."

Aish's anger beeped in and said die with her and disconnected the call.

Suraj thought no one can be more jealous than her. Jealous as she is.

Suraj always thought what's the problem with girls?

Why don't they enjoy and live the moment since we never know about the future...

Months passed by and Suraj met Aish after a long time...

Suraj had flown down to Delhi and things were not cool.

Suraj entered her home and Aish was silent. He went tpo hall and said hi to his dad and sat on a sofa watching TV.

Aish gave tea and went upstairs.

Aish was in her room and after 2 hours still, Aish didn't turn up to Suraj.

Suraj went upstairs and she was sitting on a bed, looked at her.

Anger didn't reduce in her eyes with one hand squeezing the bed sheet.

He fell to her knees and said sorry

Her anger increased still more because this was his routine whenever she was angry and tried to hold her hand

She threw his hand...

He hugged her strong and she was pushing him and tears flow in her eyes

He again hugged her saying sorry...

"Sorry baby I love you, I love you so much, you are my life, my love..."

Aish said, "You are a liar

You don't even think about me

You go where ever you want. But don't answer my calls and meet me."

"Darling, you know it's a long-distance relationship now. You stay outside the country and how shall I meet you very often?"

"Ooty is in your mind and that's very near...

roam nicely."

"Awwww"

"Hmmm" with wiping her tears

Suraj stood up, held her hands and waist and they started dancing enjoying the moves...

After a lot of cuddling, he stood up pulled her close, and dragged her one leg surrounding his lap. Held her tight and kissed her strongly for five minutes.

And after some seconds wiped her tears, it was an emotion going intimate...

He touched her lips with his fingers and smooched her again and again.

He made her lie down, she turned aside. He made her look into him

Removed his T-Shirt, trouser, and slowly removed her panty and undressed her.

Kissed her legs, slowly touched her thighs, and kissed it hardly...

He made her get up and made her touch his private part and she started sucking using her tongue and did a nice blow job and he closed his eyes and enjoyed it. He held her head tight grabbed her nearer.

She closed her eyes and got aroused when he touched her vagina...

He spread her legs and kissed her private part strongly and started licking...

He always made her comfortable and she started enjoying it and slowly whispered enough and finally, he turned her back and touched her hips with his fingers and kissed it. It got erected and he inserted his penis and fucked her hard for twenty minutes...

After emotional intercourse, he wore his

trouser back. Aish covered herself with a blanket.

He made her have some water and they hugged each other and she kissed his forehead and she smiled

Relationships always get much stronger after having a loving get together...

And yes, sex is important and it matters a lot.

But remember it should be love whatever drives you and loving moves is all that matters and yes commitment. Or else just having sex is like playing with the body. That shouldn't be the case.

Many feelings come out as we go emotional and that's the moves of love, intimacy, and sex...

Always commit to a relationship that drives the love with life long relationship.

Suraj had left his job and joined a new job and her sister Prerana was happy about it.

And Prerana was always the kind of support to his love. Whenever Suraj fought with Aish, he used to text from Prerana cell and make sure that she is ok and that way he used to take care of her.

Finally, He got engaged to Aish and they exchanged their rings and got a license of love. But it was hard for Suraj to convince his parents and hence he didn't let his parents know about it.

Some emotions were going on his mind and heart very badly and he didn’t share it with anyone. It was a very tough time and he was missing his angel badly and even Sinchu was missing him a lot and going through hard times.

But that's life. People walk into our lives and let us know about many things, we learn many things.

No one can be with us for entire life but we can keep in touch and be happy looking at their happiness from far.

And later Sinchu got married to a wonderful person and he was no less than Hrithik Roshan in his looks and Sinchu was also no less than any heroine...

Finally, Suraj's parents agreed for his marriage, and Suraj and Aish got married.

Guys and girls, everyone is the hero and heroine of their lives and creates the best happenings that you cherish forever...

Sinchu got such a nice person but he was very straight forward, reserved, and kind of a strict person but more loving...

She became busy professionally, personally, and was always I understanding with him more to have the best relationship in the future...

She was looking like a goddess in her marriage and her love enriched her beauty more and it was a memorable wedding ever.

Catch the beauty of life guys, through the love in your eyes. Understand life moves and be mature enough in handling things.

To love is nothing but take that love till marriage and having the same love after marriage is all about an everlasting love that creates happiness...

Everyone, love, live, and be happy and

mostly live your life. It's all about a matter of time and we need to be having patience in accepting the ups and downs of life...

Hope you liked and enjoyed the moves of lives and I wish everyone all the best for your future.

Catch me on with my next book to understand more about love and life.

www.ingramcontent.com/pod-product-compliance
Ingram Content Group UK Ltd.
Pitfield, Milton Keynes, MK11 3LW, UK
UKHW041820200726
13854UKWH00001BA/138